The Very Best of
OLIVIA
A Storybook Treasury

Simon Spotlight
New York   London   Toronto   Sydney   New Delhi

Contents

Dinner with OLIVIA™

adapted by Emily Sollinger   illustrated by Guy Wolek

After a busy morning at school, it was finally time for lunch. Olivia joined her friends Julian and Francine in the cafeteria.
"A cream cheese, pickle, and raisin sandwich!" Olivia announced as she opened her lunch box. She took a big bite and smiled.

Julian had a peanut butter calzone for lunch. "Want a taste?" he asked.
"I don't think so," said Olivia.
"No, thank you," said Francine as she took her lunch out of her backpack.
It was in a shiny purple box.

"What kind of lunch box is *that*?" asked Olivia.

"It's called a bento box," said Francine. "My parents got it for me in Japan!" Each compartment held a different kind of food: chicken satay, baby corn, star fruit . . . and that wasn't all. "Look at this!" Francine said proudly as she took her utensil out of the box.

"Wow," Olivia and Julian said at the same time.

"Cool spoon," said Julian.

"Cool fork!" said Olivia.

"It's both—it's a spork!" said Francine. Olivia and Julian were amazed.

Francine dug the spork into her bento box and pulled out a Brussels sprout.
"And this is a Brussels sprout. It's from Belgium . . . in Europe!"
"You *like* Brussels sprouts?" asked Julian.
"They're delicious!" Francine answered. "At my house, everything is perfectly delicious!"

Then Francine had an idea. "Olivia, you simply *must* come to my house for dinner!"

"Really? Will there be Brussels sprouts?" Olivia asked.

"Of course not!" said Francine. "We never eat the same food twice in one year."

Olivia was happy to hear that. "I'd love to come. Thank you."

"Perfect!" said Francine. "I'll have my mother call your mother."

At home that night, Olivia decided she needed to practice her manners before going to Francine's house for dinner, so she hosted her own dinner party. She reminded her guests to always say "please" and "thank you" and to put their napkins on their laps. She told them never to fall asleep at the table. She made sure they remembered to chew with their mouths closed.

"At a fancy dinner party, everything needs to be perfect!" Olivia told her guests.

Olivia imagines what dinner at Francine's house would be like. She pictures a fancy party at a mansion in the English countryside, with waiters on roller skates serving pink lemonade in tall glasses with curlicue straws and monkeys juggling fruit . . .

"Olivia! Dinnertime!" called her mother,
interrupting her daydream.

At the dinner table, Olivia's brother Ian slurped his spaghetti, splattering her dress with tomato sauce.

One of his meatballs fell to the floor, where Perry, the dog, picked it up in his mouth.

"Perry, that's *my* meatball," Ian yelled, chasing him around the table.

Perry gobbled it up . . . with his mouth open . . . leaving tomato sauce everywhere.

"I am quite sure they don't eat like this at Francine's house," Olivia groaned.

The next day, Olivia walked to Francine's house with her mother and brothers. "Have fun tonight, Olivia," her mother said, "and don't forget to invite Francine to our house for dinner too."

"OUR HOUSE?" said Olivia, horrified. She looked over at her brothers. Ian was blowing bubbles in his juice box and William's face was smeared with jam.
She imagined what dinner at her house would look like to Francine. . . .

"Welcome to our humble . . . cave!"

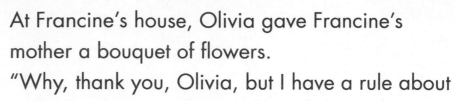

At Francine's house, Olivia gave Francine's mother a bouquet of flowers.
"Why, thank you, Olivia, but I have a rule about no fresh flowers in the house," said Francine's mother. "They make such a mess when their petals drop!"

"Be sure to wipe your feet, Olivia. We mustn't get footprints on the white carpet!"

Like any good guest, Olivia told funny stories. Just as Francine's father was telling her it wasn't polite to tell jokes at the dinner table, Olivia saw Francine's mom come out of the kitchen with bowls full of . . .

Brussels sprouts!

Olivia looked at the pile of green in her bowl. To be polite, she decided to take a very small bite. Maybe Francine was right. Maybe Brussels sprouts *were* delicious. Maybe not.

Olivia quickly reached for her water glass to wash it down but . . . Oops! She knocked one of the Brussels sprouts out of her bowl, and it rolled off the table and onto the white carpet.

Francine's mother and father were not pleased. Olivia and Francine were told to sit at the kids' table.

"Are you mad at me?" asked Francine.

"Why would I be mad?" asked Olivia.

"Because of the Brussels sprouts and the no jokes at the table," replied Francine. "And, well, I was afraid you wouldn't be my friend anymore!"

"Of *course* we're still friends!" replied Olivia. "And you should come to dinner at my house."

Later that week, it was finally Francine's turn to come to Olivia's house for dinner. It was spaghetti night. Again.

"I've never seen anyone do that before," said Francine as she watched Ian slurp his spaghetti.

"Try it!" said Ian.

"I'll race you!" said Olivia.

Turns out, Francine was a natural!

That night, as Olivia's mother tucked her into bed, Olivia had one thing on her mind. "Can we have spaghetti again tomorrow night?" she asked.

"That's a little too soon, don't you think?" said Olivia's mother.

"Okay. Good night, Mom." Olivia yawned.

"Sweet dreams, Olivia," whispered her mother as she turned off the light and closed the door.

OLIVIA™
and the Babies

adapted by Jodie Shepherd
based on the screenplay "Mother of the Year"
written by Eryk Casemiro and Kate Boutilier
illustrated by Jared Osterhold

Olivia, Ian, Baby William, and their mother had all gone to the market to shop for food.

A woman approached the shopping cart. "Coochie coochie coo," she said, tickling Baby William under his chin. "What an adorable little baby!"

"Thank you," said Mother. "Yes, he is!"

"Aren't you handsome?" another shopper said to the baby. "You should be in the movies, yes you should!"

"He is a handsome one," replied Mother. "I think I'll keep him."

"Pinto beans, garbanzo beans, beans-that-kids-should-never-have-to-eat beans," Olivia mumbled. "Mom, can we buy corn instead? Mom?"

Meanwhile, Ian was trying to decide which cereal to buy. "This one is crunchy, but there's no toy," he said to himself. "This one comes with free stick-on tattoos, but it has those gross little marshmallow things. And this one—yuck!—it gets soggy. So which should I choose? OLIVIA!"

"Look at those dimples, that smile, and oh, what a nose!" said a grocery store worker. "You must be a happy mother."

"I am," Mother answered. "Thank you."

"Ahem. M-o-m," Olivia repeated, looking at the baby. "Can we buy corn instead of beans?"

"Hmm," Olivia thought. "Baby William really *is* cute."

"Olivia, which cereal?" Ian repeated.

"I can't think about cereal right now, Ian," Olivia told her brother. "I've decided I'm going to be a mommy, and I've got a lot to do."

Back home, Olivia's new baby kept her busy. "Any letters for me, Mr. Mailman," she asked, "or for my baby, Little Olivia?"

"Oh my goodness," said the mailman. "He's a cute one, he is."

"Yes, he is cute," Olivia agreed. "I think I'll keep him."

"My, my, isn't he a vision of loveliness?" Mrs. Hogenmuller said admiringly as she passed by.

"Yes, he is," Olivia agreed again. She kissed Little Olivia on the nose. "Who's Mommy's pretty baby?" she cooed.

"One baby is so much fun," Olivia thought.

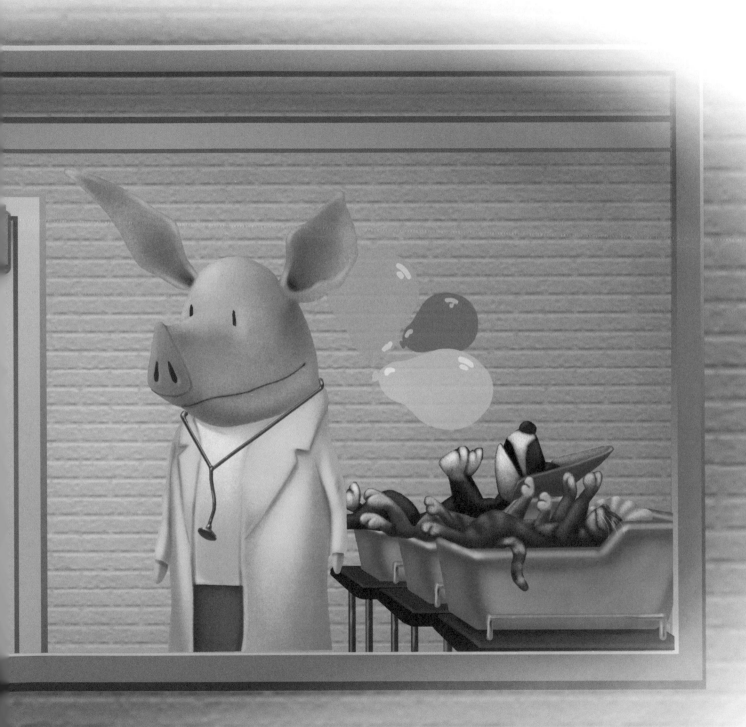

"I wonder what it would be like to have two babies. . . ."

"What would Mommy's favorite babies like to do today?" asked Olivia. "Oh, hi, Francine. I was so busy with Little Olivia and Little Olivia Two that I didn't notice you there. They're such a handful."

"Oh, wow! They're so cute," gushed Francine. "I think I'd like to be a mommy too."

"Meet Franny, my baby," said Francine. "She's a little fussy today."
"Maybe she needs a nap," Olivia suggested. "Maybe she's tired."

"It's not her naptime," Francine answered. "Babies just act fussy sometimes."

"Hey, Olivia!" shouted Francine. "Make your babies behave! Your babies are causing trouble."

"Little Olivia Two, get back in your carriage!" Olivia said firmly. She turned to Francine. "He's not misbehaving; he is just getting some exercise."

"HELP!" Francine shouted. "Franny, come to Mommy!"
Olivia stayed calm. "I'm sorry to say this, Francine, but I think it would be best
if Franny didn't play with my babies today."
"Bye, Olivia!" said Francine.

Back home, Olivia had just put her babies down for a nap when Mother asked for her help.
Olivia agreed to watch William while her mother was on the phone . . . as long as she could call him Little Olivia Three.
William didn't seem to mind.

Just when everything was peaceful, Ian came into the room and woke
up all three babies.
"Now how am I going to take care of all my babies at the same time?"
Olivia thought. Then she had an idea . . .

Roller skates!

Little Olivia Three was in tears.

"Wheee! Wheee!" called Olivia. "Look at me, Little Olivia Three!"
Little Olivia Three stopped crying and started to giggle! Mommies
can be so silly!

That night Olivia was really tired!
"I'm really proud of you, Olivia,"
said Mother.
"Thank you, Mom," Olivia
replied. "But being a mommy
is a lot of work. I think I'll wait
until I'm old—like you."
Mother smiled. "And I'm sure
when you have
babies of your own
you will be mother
of the year! Good
night, Olivia."

OLIVIA™
Opens a Lemonade Stand

adapted by Kama Einhorn

based on the screenplay by Eryk Casemiro and Kate Boutilier

illustrated by Jared Osterhold

It was a hot summer day, and Olivia was busy opening up her very own lemonade stand. Ian and Julian helped make the lemonade. They squeezed lemon juice into a pitcher of water, added sugar, and stirred.

"Fresh-squeezed lemonade," Olivia said. "Everyone's going to want to buy some of this. I've dreamed of opening a lemonade stand my whole life!"

"Olivia's Lemony Lemonade stand is open for business!" declared Olivia.
She poured a cup for Julian. "Now I need you to be totally honest,"
she said. "Isn't it delicious?"
"S . . . s . . . sour!" gasped Julian.
"Well, lemonade is *supposed* to be sour," said Olivia.

Then Olivia tried the lemonade herself. Ack! "Okay, it's a little sour," she admitted. "I'd better fix this before customers get here. Ian, go fill this cup with sugar and bring it back."

"Say please," said Ian.

"Please," said Olivia. "Now *please* hurry!"

Ian went to the kitchen and called out to his mother.
"Where's the sugar?" he asked.
"In the cabinet, next to the salt," she answered.

Ian rushed the cup back to Olivia, who added it to the lemonade just in time to say, "Good morning, Mrs. Hoggenmuller! Would you like a cup of my Lemony Lemonade?"

"Yes, please," said Mrs. Hoggenmuller. "Oh, there's nothing more delightful than a delicious glass of lemonade on a hot summer's day. In fact, I'll take two."

"What do you think?" asked Olivia.

"Mmmm-gggg-phhhh . . . too . . . salty!" cried Mrs. Hoggenmuller.
"Wow, look at her face!" said Harold, who had stopped by with Daisy.

"Is your lemonade sour? We love anything super-sour," said Daisy.
"Yep. That's why I call it Olivia's Super-Sour Lemonade! You've come to the right place!" said Olivia.
They both took a sip. "Ugh! Salty!" said Harold.
"It tastes like the ocean," said Daisy.

"Ian! You gave me salt, not sugar!" Olivia cried.

"Oops!" Ian said. "Sorry, they're both white."

"This is my Super-Sour-Kind-of-Salty one, but I have two other pitchers of Super-Sour Lemonade coming right up," Olivia assured her customers.

Then Olivia saw Francine next door in her driveway, calling out "Fresh strawberry lemonade! Get your strawberry lemonade here! It's pink and yummy—and *unsalted*!"

When Francine noticed Olivia, she said, "Oh, hello there, Olivia. Would you like some strawberry lemonade?"

"No, thank you," said Olivia. "I have my *own* lemonade stand."

"I'll be right back with more paper cups, everybody," said Francine proudly. "I had no idea it would be such a hit!"

Now Francine had lots of customers, and Olivia had none. "I don't want a lemonade stand anymore anyway," Olivia told Julian.
"But, Olivia—you've wanted one your whole life!" said Julian.
"I mean . . . I don't want *just* a lemonade stand anymore," she said. I wonder what it would be like to have my very own restaurant . . . , Olivia thought.

It's Olivia's . . . Olivia's Restaurant! Thanks for coming,
it sure does mean a lot.
Welcome to Olivia's, where the food is delicious and
everything is served with Super-Sour Lemonade!

"We've got work to do . . . in my *new restaurant*!" Olivia told her staff. "Come on!"

"If I'm cooking and Julian's walking around with a towel on his arm, what are you doing?" Ian asked Olivia.

"It's my restaurant," explained Olivia patiently. "My job is to walk around and sing and make sure people are having fun. Oh—customers!" she cried. "Ian, start cooking. Julian, start doing waiter stuff."

"Good afternoon, Daisy. Hello, Harold. Welcome to Olivia's Restaurant," said Olivia.

"The cracker and banana appetizer is very good tonight. Your waiter will be right with you. To start, here are two cups of Olivia's Super-Sour Salt-Free Lemonade."

"Mmm, really sour," said Daisy.

"I can hardly move my tongue," said Harold happily.

"I'm supposed to tell you that this is today's special: Fruity cereal nuggets with gravy," Julian said. "I'll be right back with the main course . . . uh, spaghetti and raisins."

"This is the best restaurant ever!" said Daisy.

Oscar and Otto came by too. "Hi, Oscar. Hi, Otto. I hope this table is okay," Olivia said.
She noticed an angry squirrel was in the tree above, dropping acorns on her customers. But Oscar and Otto didn't mind.
"Oh no, we like it," said Oscar.
"It's cool," said Otto.

Ian stayed busy cooking in the kitchen. "Look, Mom, I'm a chef!" he said proudly.

Sophie and Caitlin came by next.

"Excuse me. Do you have any sour pink grapefruit jelly beans?" Sophie asked.

"How about pink marshmallow watermelon kebobs?" asked Caitlin.

"They only eat or drink pink food," Julian explained to Olivia.

"Pink food?" said Olivia. "That's the one thing we don't have!"

Olivia knew just what to do. She went straight to Francine. "Two glasses of your strawberry lemonade, please," she said. "It's for some customers at my restaurant. Francine poured the glasses and also gave Olivia some for herself. "This is really good, Francine," Olivia told her.

"Thank you," said Francine. "But running a lemonade stand isn't as much fun as I thought."

"Having a restaurant is lots more fun," said Olivia.

"If you're tired of the same old juice box, then come to Olivia's restaurant, home of Francine's Strawberry Lemonade," Olivia announced. Then she looked at her band. "Hit it!" she said.

"We're Olivia's—and Francine's Pink Strawberry Lemonade! Oh, yeah!"

And so Olivia and Francine became partners. Running a restaurant was hard work, but it was really fun when everyone did it together.

That night, after her bedtime story, Olivia was still thinking about her restaurant.
She handed her mother a new book to read.
"But this is a cookbook," Mother said. "It could take all night to read a cookbook.
How about we save it for tomorrow?"

"Well . . . all right," agreed Olivia. "Good night, Mom."
"Good night, sweetie."

OLIVIA
and the Haunted Hotel

adapted by Jodie Shepherd
based on the screenplay
"OLIVIA Plays Hotel"
written by Kate Boutilier and
Eryk Casemiro

illustrated by Patrick Spaziante

"Look at all that rain!" exclaimed Olivia. "Thunder and lightning, too. I love spooky weather!"

81

"Did you have fun at school today?" asked Mother.
Before anyone could answer there was an enormous *BOOM* of thunder.
Ian and Olivia yelled, "Wooohoo!"

"I know the perfect game to play when we get to my house," said Olivia.

"Welcome to the Hotel Olivia," Olivia greets her guests.

"Please come in and make yourselves at home."

"Wow, it's so big!" Francine says.

"This is nothing," answers Olivia. "You should see my other hotels."

Olivia's house made a perfect hotel.

"I'd like a room, please," Francine requested.

"Me too," said Julian. "I mean a different room. Maybe one with a TV."

"Of course," Olivia replied politely. "That shouldn't be a problem."

There was a flash of lightning. *Whooo! Tap, tap, tap.*

The wind whistled and tree branches tapped on the windowpanes.

"What was that sound?" asked Julian nervously.

"Sounds like a ghost," Francine said, trembling.

"Ghost? The Hotel Olivia has no ghosts," Olivia answered firmly.

"Follow me, please."

"This is your room, Francine," said Olivia, opening a door.

"No offense, Olivia," said Francine, "but I'd like another room. This one smells like boy."

"I'll take it," said Julian. "I already smell like boy. Does it come with room service?"

"Of course," Olivia answered, opening the door to a second room. "All our rooms do. They also come with fluffy towels and chocolates on the pillows. That's what makes the Hotel Olivia the fanciest hotel in the world."

"I love my new room!" cried Francine. "This is the best hotel ever!"

Brring! A bell rang from downstairs.

"Excuse me," said Olivia. "I think I have another customer."

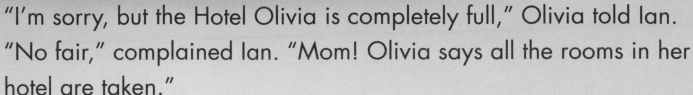

"I'm sorry, but the Hotel Olivia is completely full," Olivia told Ian. "No fair," complained Ian. "Mom! Olivia says all the rooms in her hotel are taken."

"Olivia, I'm sure you can find a room for Ian *somewhere* in your large hotel," said Mother.

"This is our last room," Olivia announced. "You'll love the privacy. Plus the soaps are free. But you'll have to leave when the other guests need to use the bathroom."

"Never mind. I don't want to stay at this hotel anyway," said Ian. "Besides, I heard there were ghosts."

"Ghosts!" repeated Francine and Julian.

Room service kept Olivia very busy—too busy to play with her brother.
She delivered lunches,

made beds,

cleaned up dog toys,

and soothed frightened guests.
"It's just the hotel laundry," reassured
Olivia.

That gave Ian an idea.

Suddenly there was a loud bang and everything went dark.

"HEY! WHO TURNED OUT THE LIGHTS?" yelled Francine, alarmed.

"The storm must have knocked the power out," guessed Julian.

"Or a ghost did," whispered Francine.
"I told you, Francine," said Olivia, "there are no ghosts at this hotel."

"BOO!"

"Aah! Ghost!" screamed Francine.

"Aah! I see it too!" screamed Julian.

"Where? There are no ghosts at the Hotel Olivia,"
Olivia repeated.

Francine and Julian huddled together. "Well, I saw a ghost," said Francine, "and I don't want to stay in this spooky hotel anymore." "Me neither," Julian agreed. "This hotel is haunted."

HMM. If I do have a ghost in my hotel, then I'm just going to have to get rid of it, Olivia thinks. Good thing I have a Ghost-o-Meter.

"I *knew* it was you, Ian!" said Olivia. Then she called downstairs.

"Mom, Ian is scaring my guests."

"Well, Olivia, maybe Ian just wants to play," Mother called back.

"Hmm," said Olivia. "I know! Ian, how would you like to be the room-service waiter?"

"Cool!" said Ian.

"Welcome to breakfast at the ghost-free Hotel Olivia," said Ian the next morning. "Today we are serving our world-famous pancakes."

"Yum," said Francine.

"Double yum," said Julian.

"More pancakes, anyone?" asked Mother.

OLIVIA™

and the School Carnival

adapted by Tina Gallo
based on the screenplay "OLIVIA
Runs a Carnival"
written by Joe Purdy

illustrated by Guy Wolek

"In a few days, our class will be hosting parents' night," said Mrs. Hoggenmuller. "Let's put our thinking caps on and come up with fun activities for the evening. Harold? Do you have any ideas?" she asked.

"We can have a finger-painting party! Only you paint with your feet!" he said.

"Thank you, Harold, I will keep that in mind," Mrs. Hoggenmuller said. "Anyone else? Olivia? Do you have an idea?" Mrs. Hoggenmuller asked.

"We could make our own carnival!" Olivia said. "We could have games, and rides, and prizes!"

Olivia's classmates loved her idea. And so did Mrs. Hoggenmuller. "What a fantastic idea," she said. "And Olivia, I'd love for you to be in charge—with my supervision of course."

Olivia imagined what it would be like to be the ringmaster in a carnival. . . .
"Step right up, everyone, and come see the best, the biggest, the most fun
carnival ever made!" Ringmaster Olivia shouted to the excited crowd.

The next day at school, Olivia placed her classmates in groups of three to make up their own booth or game for the carnival.

"How is the Ring Toss game coming along?" Olivia asked Francine's group.

"Oh sorry, Olivia," Francine said. "I decided a ring toss was too boring. So we changed it to a Pin-the-Nose-on-the-Clown game."

"I like it a lot!" Olivia said. "But what if you did something like . . ." Olivia leaned in close and whispered so only Francine could hear.

"What a great idea!" Francine said.

Next, Olivia visited Julian's group.
She stared at the brightly colored tunnel in front of her and wondered what it was.
"We call it the Roly-Twisty Tunnel Ride," Connor explained. "Watch."

Julian crawled inside the tunnel and Connor and Daisy rolled it back and forth
across the floor. When the ride was over, Julian could barely stand up straight.
"I'm not so sure about this," Julian said. "It makes you kind of dizzy. Whoa."
"It looks like fun to me!" Olivia said. "But it might be even MORE fun if you
tried. . ." And she whispered so only Daisy, Connor, and Julian could hear.
All three of them loved Olivia's idea. They couldn't wait to try it out!

Finally, Olivia checked on Harold's group. She saw a frog sitting in the middle of a bunch of toys. "So your attraction is The World's Largest Frog?" Olivia asked. "Yes. See how it works? He looks pretty big next to these toys," Alexandra explained.

Before Olivia could say another word, the frog jumped and sat on Harold's head. Harold turned and asked Alexandra, "He won't be doing that on parents' night, will he? My mom freaks out about frogs."

"Your attraction is really great," Olivia said. "But I wonder if this might make it even better . . ." She leaned in close to whisper.

"Can you whisper your idea again?" Harold asked. "It's hard to pay attention when there's a frog on your head."

Olivia took the frog off Harold's head and whispered her suggestion right in Harold's ear. He loved it!

When class was over, Mrs. Hoggenmuller spoke to Olivia. "Olivia, everyone is thrilled with your suggestions!" she said. "It looks like you're doing an excellent job as carnival director."

"Thank you, Mrs. Hoggenmuller," Olivia replied.

"And how is your own special attraction coming along?" Mrs. Hoggenmuller asked.

"Well, I have lots of ideas, but I haven't decided which one should be my extra special attraction," Olivia said.

Mrs. Hoggenmuller smiled. "Well don't worry, dear. Great ideas have a way of sneaking up on you."

On her way home, Olivia imagined she was surrounded by reporters with microphones and cameras. . . .

"Olivia, can we see your extra special, top-secret attraction now?" asks one reporter.

"Yes, Olivia, what's under the sheet?" asks another reporter.

"Only the soon-to-be most-talked-about, most-pictures-taken-of, world-famous, most amazing attraction ever built!" Olivia says.

"Show us, Olivia!" begs a third reporter.

"Sorry, but it's not ready for the public yet. You'll have to come back tomorrow, at parents' night," Olivia tells them.

That night, Olivia told her parents about her project. She showed her dad the sketches she had made of all of her ideas.

"Okay, Dad, here's how my extra special project is going to work. . . ."

Olivia's father looked at all the sketches carefully. "Hmmm, classic design, very scientific, it pushes, it pulls . . . You just might need a little help."

Olivia's brother Ian walked into the living room. He was holding his favorite toy robot. Ian began speaking in a robotic voice.

"Why-don't-you-ask-the-boy-standing-next-to-you?" Ian asked in his best robot voice.

"Okay, you can help," Olivia said.

Ian turned to his parents. "See-you-later-parents-of-Robot-Boy."

The big night finally arrived. Mrs. Hoggenmuller greeted the parents. "Welcome to parents' night!

Olivia beamed. "Thank you, Mrs. Hoggenmuller! Folks, follow me to view our first attraction, which was made by Francine, Oscar, and Otto. It's the one, the only, Amazing Clown Beanbag Toss! Would someone care to try it?"

Next Olivia walked over to what used to be the Roly-Twisty Tunnel Ride. "Here we have Beach Ball Bowling," Olivia announced. "All you have to do is throw a ball through the tunnel and out the other side to knock down these bowling pins! Julian, will you demonstrate?"
Everybody cheered for Julian's strike.

Olivia walked over to the next attraction. "And step this way, ladies and gentlemen, and see The Most Strange Animal of All Time . . . the last living dinosaur, the frogosaurus! Watch it climb up a tall building!"

Harold stood behind a model of the Empire State Building and let the frogosaurus go. It hopped up the building and then right on his head again! "It's okay, Mom, it doesn't bite!" Harold said.

"And finally, for our last attraction," Olivia said, "welcome to Olivia's Spectacular Fun House!"

Olivia pointed to the fun house behind her. "I couldn't have done it without my little brother Ian!"

Ian peeked his head out from behind a flap in the fun house. "She's right, she couldn't have!"

Olivia stood in front of the fun house mirrors. "Now watch carefully as the Hall of Mirrors transforms an ordinary boy into . . . The Amazing Robot Boy!"
Ian placed his toy robot in front of the mirrors.
The mirrors made Ian's toy robot look huge! Now it looked like a real robot boy.
All the parents laughed and cheered.

Mrs. Hoggenmuller walked over next to Olivia. "Great job, everyone!" she said. "Parents, enjoy the carnival!"

That night, when her mom tucked her into bed, Olivia was very sleepy, but very happy.

"I really want to show you my idea for a carnival booth," Olivia said.

Olivia's mom smiled. "I would love to look at your idea, Olivia . . . in the morning."

"But my idea glows in the dark, so it's really best if we talk about it now!" Olivia explained.

"Your idea will still be there in the morning. Good night, Olivia. Sweet dreams, honey."

"Good night, Mom."

OLIVIA™
Cooks Up a Surprise

adapted by Emily Sollinger
based on the screenplay "OLIVIA Becomes a Chef" written by Pat Resnick
illustrated by Jared Osterhold

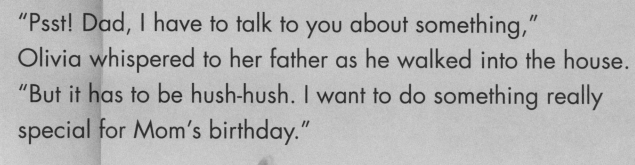

"Psst! Dad, I have to talk to you about something," Olivia whispered to her father as he walked into the house. "But it has to be hush-hush. I want to do something really special for Mom's birthday."

129

"Great idea!" said Father. "Do you want to make her a card?
Or a present?"
"I want to cook a surprise dinner for her!"
"I'll make peanut-butter-and-chocolate sandwiches," Ian offered
excitedly.

"Ian! You have to *double* promise not to tell her!" Olivia explained.

"I'll *triple* promise," said Ian. "But I want to help!"

"We'll all help," said Father. "But how can we get her out of the house while we cook?"

"Just leave that to me," Olivia said with a smile.

Olivia picked up the phone and dialed her grandma's number.

"Hello?" answered Grandma.

"Grandma! It's Secret Agent Olivia here. I need your help on a tip-top secret mission."

"Agent Grandma, at your service."

"Your mission is to get Mom out of the house on her birthday so we can cook her a special surprise fancy dinner!" Olivia explained. "Mission accomplished," answered Grandma.

On the morning of Mother's birthday, Olivia and Ian rushed into the kitchen with homemade cards. "Happy birthday, Mom!" they shouted happily.

"Thank you so much! I can't wait to spend the whole day with my marvelous family!" Mother said.

At that moment the doorbell rang. *Ding-dong!*

"Whoever that is," said Mother, "they are not going to interrupt my special day with my family."

"*Surprise!*" Olivia's grandma called out as she walked through the door. "It's your birthday and I'm taking you shopping! Just the two of us!"

"But—," Mother tried to get a word in.

"No buts!" interrupted Grandma.

"But . . . ," repeated Mother.

"Grandma's orders! Let's go!"

"Bye!" called Olivia as her grandma rushed her mom out the door.

Once Mother was out of the house, Olivia, Ian, and Father headed straight to the grocery store.

"This one is magnificent!" said Olivia as she picked up a watermelon. "Now on to the red peppers!"

"I sense a red theme for this dinner," said Father.

"Yes, *very* red. And *very* fancy. Red is the very best color for *everything*," Olivia explained. She picked out the reddest red peppers, red tomatoes, and red radishes.

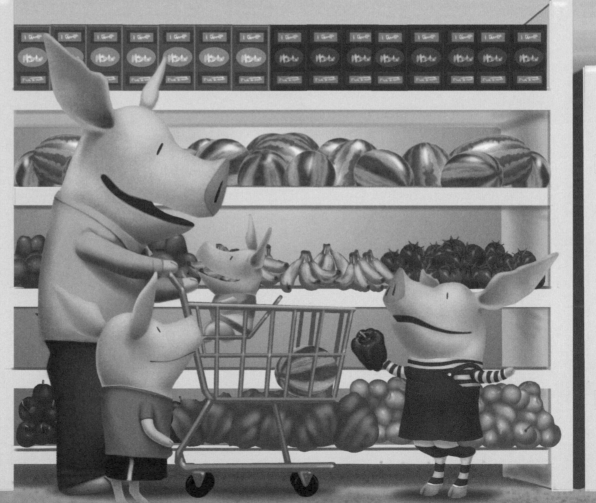

Back at home Olivia, Ian, and Father unloaded the groceries.
"Are we all set to begin, Chef Olivia?" asked Father once everything
was unpacked.
"Who's ready to make some kitchen magic?" asked Olivia. "Dad,
please heat the water for the pasta and peel the tomatoes. Ian, please
measure two cups of flour and put butter in the bowl."
"Wait! I'm still putting water in the pot! What was the next step?"
asked Father frantically.
"Did you say to put butter in the tomatoes?" Ian asked.

"It needs some more strawberry jam," Olivia muttered to herself, mixing in a large bowl.
"Now it's ready for the oven!" she announced proudly as her dad helped her place a cake pan in the oven. She admired her cake through the oven window. "Smell the aroma. See the red velvetiness. And now . . . the taste test!"

Olivia offered a taste to Ian and her dad. "This is definitely, absolutely the best thing I have ever had!" they both said at the same time.

"Excellent!" said Olivia. "On to the next course!"

141

"Okay. Salad? Done. Spaghetti sauce? Done. Red velvet cake? Just needs red frosting," Olivia announced.
"I thought you were going to put all of those ingredients into *one* dish," said Ian.

"That's a good idea, Ian! Next time we should *definitely* do that," giggled Olivia.

"Come on, Ian. Let's clean up this mess before Mom gets home!" said Olivia. They washed the dishes and cleaned the counters. They put away the ingredients and swept the floor.

Before long, the kitchen was sparkling clean. Mother wouldn't suspect a thing!

Just as they finished cleaning up, Olivia's mom and grandma came through the front door.

"I was sure shopping would take hours," Grandma explained. "But I missed my family," said Olivia's mom, smiling.

"Do you want to take a birthday rest?" Olivia's dad asked.

"No," answered her mom.

"*Sure* you do," insisted her grandma. "I know *I'm* tired."

"Go ahead," said her dad. "I'll bring you some water."

"But—," Olivia's mom tried to get a word in.

"Grandma's orders!" said Grandma.

Once Mother was out of sight, Olivia and Ian carefully set the table. Once the table was all set, Olivia called out to her mom.
"Mom! Come on in!"
Mother smiled as she walked into the dining room.
"Surprise! Happy birthday!" everyone shouted.

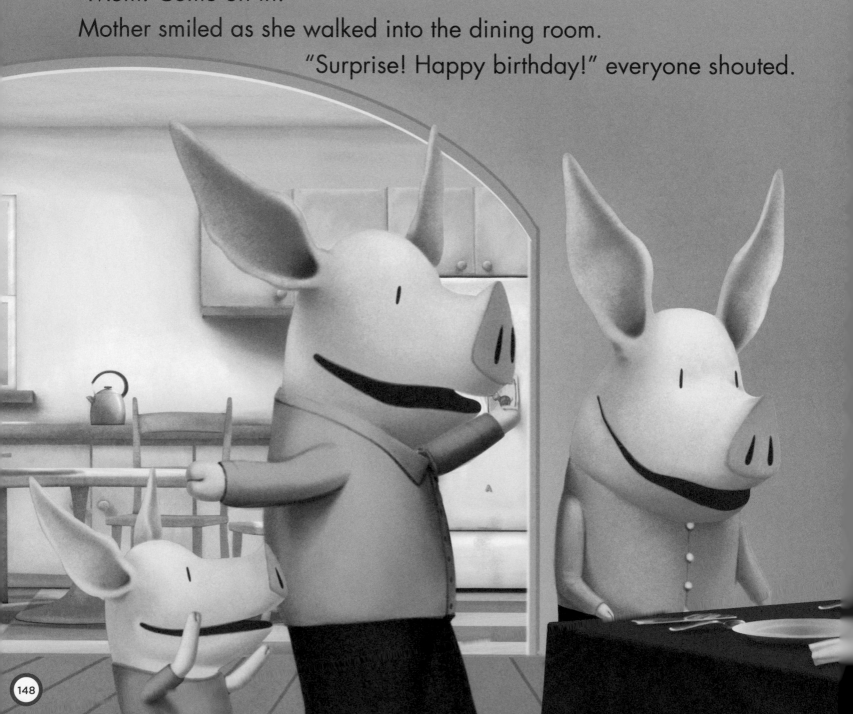

"Your birthday dinner is served! We made all of your favorites," Olivia explained.

"Except peanut-butter-and-chocolate sandwiches because they aren't red," said Ian.

"What a perfect surprise!" said Olivia's mother. "You made my birthday so special! And now I understand why you wanted me out of the house, and out of the kitchen!"

"We love you, Mom," said Olivia and Ian.

"Thank you again for making dinner and for cleaning up the kitchen," Olivia's mother said as she tucked her in that night. "You are a *most* amazing daughter."

"Thanks, Mom. And how am I as a chef?" asked Olivia sleepily.

"Beyond amazing. A magician in the kitchen!" said her mom.

"Happy birthday, Mom. Good night," whispered Olivia.

"Good night, sweetheart," Mother whispered back.

OLIVIA™
Leads a Parade

adapted by Kama Einhorn
based on the screenplay
written by Pat Resnick

illustrated by Shane L. Johnson

"Ah, nothing like watching a parade from the comfort of your own couch," said Olivia to her dad as they watched a parade on television.

"I want to play that huge drum!" said Julian.

"Look at the floats!" said Ian.

"And the majorettes!" Olivia added. "I'd like to be the one twirling the baton. . . ."

Olivia imagined herself as a marching majorette . . .
spinning her baton . . .
tossing it into the air . . .
twirling around . . .
and doing a split.
TA-DA!

"I wish we could have parades like that in our town," said Ian.

Olivia had a brilliant idea. "Ian, we can have our *own* parade!"

"Great!" said Julian and Ian.

They went right to work. "Julian, you can be the marching band," declared Olivia. "Ian, you can play the cymbals. And I'm the majorette—this ruler is my baton! Now, all together!"

Everyone began to march in place. *BAM, CRASH, BOOM!* went the parade band, and Perry howled along.

Upstairs, Olivia's mother was trying to get baby William to take his nap. She poked her head out of the window and called down, "Kids, could you play your music a little more quietly?"

"WHAT, MOM?" shouted Olivia.

"William needs his nap!" her mom answered.

"Oops. Sorry, Mom," Olivia and Ian said.

They went inside to look for things they could use in a quiet parade. Olivia found an old pennant from a baseball game.

"Pennants! Pennants are quiet," she said. She started making a pretty new pennant from the old one.

"Just needs a little glue," she said. "Perfect!"

But the glue stuck to Olivia's hand. "Uh-oh! It's stuck!" she said, and they all giggled.

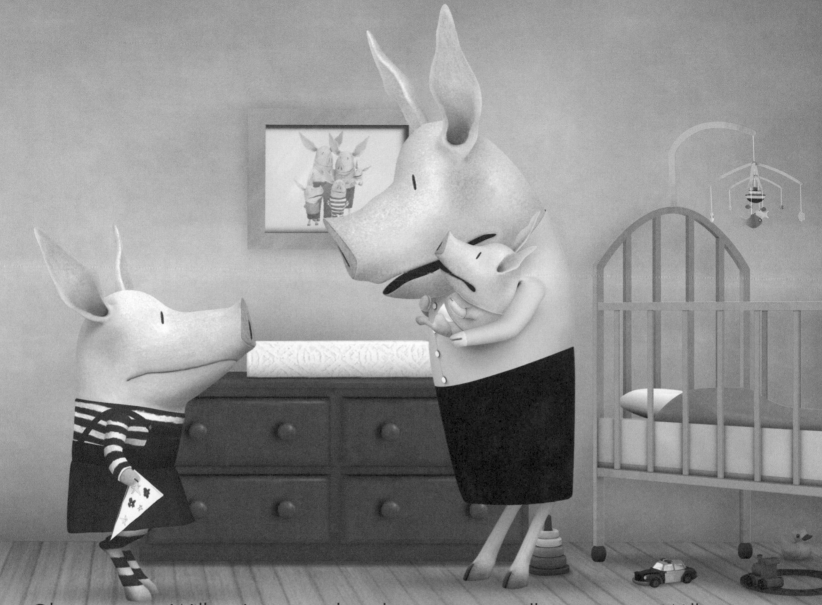

Olivia ran into William's room, where her mom was still trying to get William to fall asleep.

"Mom, I need a little help!" Olivia said loudly.

William cried loudly. He had just fallen asleep, and now he was awake again.

"Olivia, I asked you to keep the noise down," her mother sighed. "Maybe he'd like some fresh air," she said. She picked William up to take him outside.

Olivia, Ian, and Julian went outside to try again.

"Okay, let's take it from the top!" Olivia announced. "Shhh, the cymbals are too loud, Ian. But can you do tricks on your tricycle?" she suggested. "Okay, parade, get ready to march! One, two, three, go!"

The three marched along proudly until Olivia's baton got stuck in the tree. Then Ian crashed his tricycle loudly into the garbage cans. This parade was not very quiet.

Just then, Francine and Alexandra came by. "What's making all that noise?" asked Francine.

"Shhh!" said Olivia. "Hi, Francine. Hi, Alexandra," she whispered. "We need to be quiet because my baby brother is trying to nap."

"What are you guys doing?" asked Alexandra.

"We're having a parade," said Julian. "Want to be in it?"

Francine seemed interested. "What kind of parade?"

"A fabulous parade," Olivia promised. "But we have to be very quiet."

"The parade will begin here," Olivia explained. "I'll be in the front twirling my baton. Julian will be leading the drummers here. Ian, you'll ride your tricycle here. Francine and Alexandra, you can pull the float back here."
Francine paused. "I think the parade should have clowns in it." She added a clown to the drawing.

"I'm not really a clown person," Olivia told Francine.

"Really?" Francine said. "Well, I'm a clown person! I'll lead my own parade. *With* clowns. Come on, Alexandra." And they left.

"Don't worry, our parade will be much better," Olivia reassured Julian and Ian.

Soon Olivia's mom came to say hello. William was wide-awake and squirmy.

"How are you kids doing?" she asked.

"Great," said Olivia. "Mom, you should take William for a drive," she suggested. "He always falls asleep in the car."

"I wish I could," her mom said. "But I have too much work to catch up on. And besides, I wouldn't want to miss the parade."

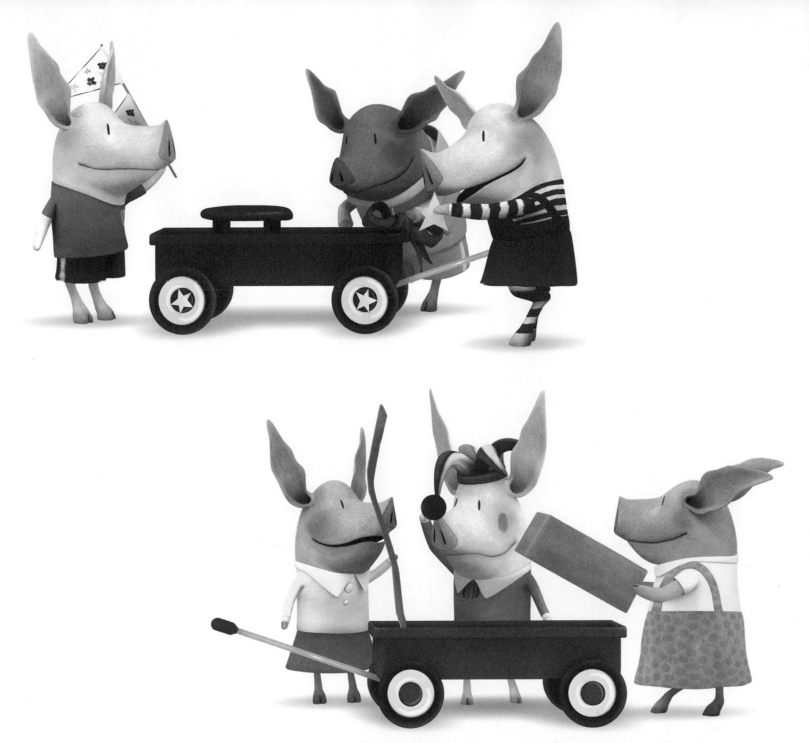

"Okay, let's decorate the float!" Olivia exclaimed. Francine and her friends decorated their float too, and Francine got into her clown costume.

Both parades marched along the sidewalk until they bumped right into each other.

"Excuse me, Olivia," Francine said. "My parade needs to get through."

"But we thought of the parade first," Olivia pointed out. Then she had an idea.

Olivia imagined a fabulous parade with all of her friends. Wouldn't one big parade be better than two medium-size parades?

"Come on, let's join parades!" Olivia said to Francine.
Francine thought about it and talked to her friends. "Okay," she agreed.
"But I'm not changing out of my clown costume."
"Okay, follow my lead everybody!" said Olivia.

Several people had already gathered on the sidewalk to watch the parade.
"Let the parade begin!" Olivia exclaimed loudly. Then she saw her mom
holding William.
"I have an idea! Can William ride in the parade too?" she asked her mom.
Her mom smiled and shrugged. "Why not? He's not sleeping anyway!"

Now Olivia was ready. "Follow my lead, everybody.
William says, 'Let the parade begin!'"
And it did.

It was a very noisy parade.
William fell asleep right away.
It was a wonderful parade.

"Thank you for getting William to sleep today," Olivia's mom said as she tucked her in. "It was a great parade."

Olivia yawned. "I think I'm only going to have a parade once every five years because they're so much work," she said sleepily. "No books tonight, Mom."

"Wow, you must really be tired," her mom said.

"I'll have double books tomorrow," Olivia reassured her. "Good night."

"Good night, Olivia."

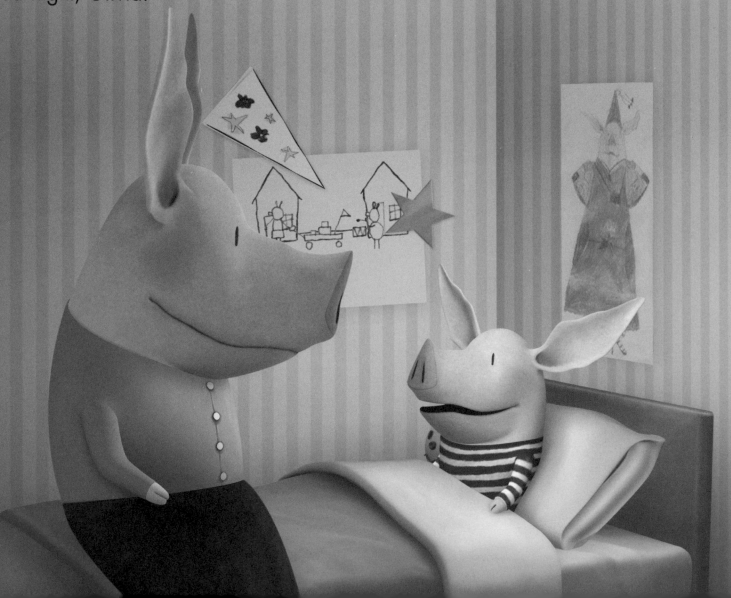

OLIVIA
the Princess

adapted by Natalie Shaw
based on the screenplay written by Kent Redeker
illustrated by Shane L. Johnson

Olivia, Francine, and Daisy were playing princess when Mom rushed in with exciting news. The royal family of Poshtonia was coming to town to visit their vacation castle, and everyone was invited to greet them at the airport!

"A real king and queen?" asked Olivia.

"And a real princess, Princess Stephanie," added Mom.

The next day everyone cheered as the royal airplane rolled to a stop, but Olivia was pushed to the back of the crowd and couldn't see. In a flash the princess climbed into the royal carriage behind the king and queen, and it sped away. "The princess was so beautiful!" said Francine. "Did you see that dress?" "I saw her back, I think," said Olivia.

On the way home, Dad and Mom tried to cheer Olivia up.

"Well, do you know what's even better than princesses?" Dad asked.

"Cherry chocolate chunk ice cream!" Olivia said.

"That's just what I was thinking," said Dad.

They drove to the ice-cream parlor. Just as they were about to go inside they heard someone ask for help. It was the king of Poshtonia!

"It seems our carriage has broken a wheel, but none of us knows how to fix it," said the king.

"Well, Mr. King, sir, I think I can help," Dad said. He turned to Mom and the queen. "This could take a while. Maybe *your highnesses* would like to take everyone inside for some ice cream?"

"Did someone say ice cream?" said a voice coming from the carriage. Olivia gasped. It was Princess Stephanie! As they headed inside, Olivia and the princess stared at each other.

"You look just like me!" they both said.

The princess had freckles and Olivia's ears were bigger, but other than that they could have been twins!

As soon as they ordered their ice cream, Olivia asked Princess Stephanie what it was like to be a real princess. "What do you do first in the morning?" she asked. "Ride a pony or have tea?"

The princess was about to answer when she spilled a tiny drop of ice cream onto her royal dress.

"My dress!" she said. "A princess must never have a messy dress."

"I'll help you clean up," said Olivia.

"I bet you get to wear pretty dresses like this to fancy balls," said Olivia. "I've never even been to a ball!"

"Well, you get to go to school and play with other children," replied Princess Stephanie. "I wish I could do that, even for a day."

Then Olivia had an idea. "We look so much alike. We should switch places for the day!" she suggested.

The princess was thinking the same thing! They quickly changed into each other's clothes and agreed to have their parents bring them back to the ice-cream parlor the following night, so they could switch back again.

When it was time for everyone to go home, the king thanked Olivia's dad for helping him fix the carriage wheel.

"Getting my hands dirty was most thrilling!" said the king.

"It's been a pleasure, your majesty!" said Olivia's dad as he bowed.

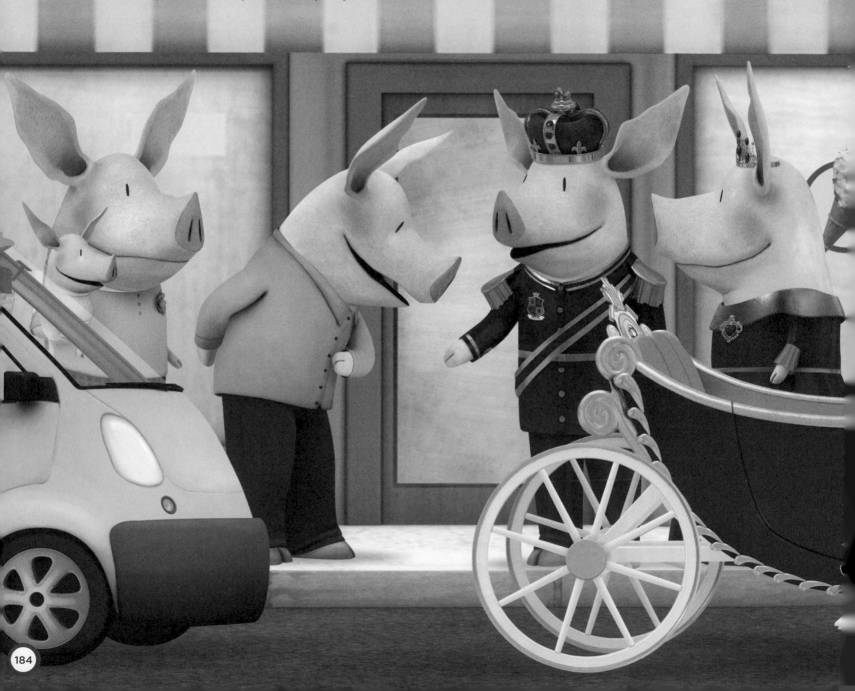

"See you later, *Olivia*!" Olivia said as she climbed into the royal carriage, dressed in Princess Stephanie's purple gown.

"Ta-ta, *Princess Stephanie*," said Princess Stephanie as she climbed into Olivia's family's car, dressed in Olivia's red clothes.

They were on their way! Olivia went to the castle to spend a day as a princess, and Princess Stephanie went to Olivia's house to spend a day as a regular girl.

When they arrived at the castle, Olivia was in awe. There were turrets and towers and even a drawbridge!

She rode Duchess the pony across the royal lawn, slid down the royal banister, and had a royal tea party.

She even had her own butler!

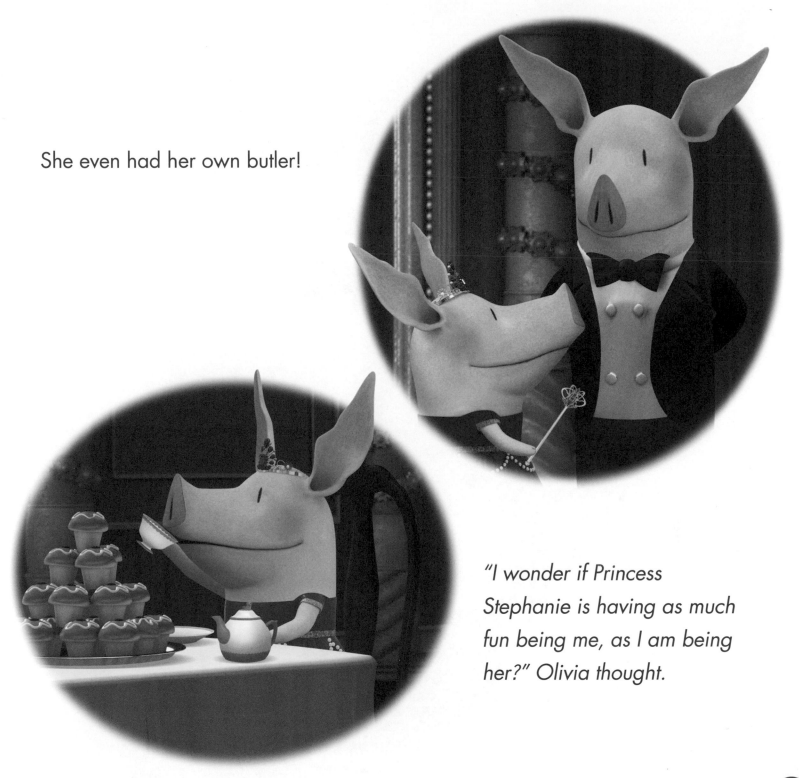

"I wonder if Princess Stephanie is having as much fun being me, as I am being her?" Olivia thought.

Back at Olivia's house, Princess Stephanie played fetch with Perry and banged on the drums.

"Look at me. I'm getting dirty and making noise!" she said. "How marvelous!"

When Olivia's family sat down for dinner, Princess Stephanie asked if they would be having pheasant on a silver platter. Mom laughed and set down a paper plate with a sandwich on it.

"A sandwich! On a paper plate!" said Princess Stephanie, with a big smile. "How delightful!"

After a long day it was time for Olivia and Princess Stephanie to go to bed. They both missed their real parents very much, but they knew that they would be back home soon.

At the castle the next morning, the queen announced that they had to return home to Poshtonia sooner than planned.

"But we have to go to the ice-cream parlor tonight after dinner!" said Olivia. If they couldn't go to the ice-cream parlor as planned, Olivia needed to find a way to get Princess Stephanie back to castle so they could switch places again.

"Let's have a going-away party before we leave!" she said. "We could invite that nice girl from the ice-cream parlor, and my—I mean—*her* whole class, too!" The queen agreed and sent the royal butler to deliver invitations to Olivia's classmates and their families.

Before long, the guests arrived and the going-away party was in full swing. Olivia was happy to see her friends, but it wasn't very much fun because they thought she was Princess Stephanie. She was ready to be Olivia again!

When the clock struck four, the king and queen announced that it was time to go home to Poshtonia, but Olivia's family hadn't arrived yet. Olivia knew that if she didn't speak now, she'd have to go back to Poshtonia with the royal family.

"There's something I have to tell you," she said. "I'm Olivia, not Princess Stephanie! We switched places. Look, I have bigger ears and no freckles and I'm wearing red-and-white stockings."

The queen let out a gasp. "Princess! You're not wearing purple!" she said.
"This jest has gone on long enough. We have to get on our plane. Now, pledge
to me that you'll behave like a proper princess," said the king.
That reminded Olivia of the Princess Pledge that she had made up.
"That's it! The Princess Pledge!" she said to Francine and Daisy.
"There's no such thing as a princess pledge," said the queen.

"Maybe not in Poshtonia," Olivia said. "But there is one here in Maywood!"

Olivia began to say the Princess Pledge, and Francine and Daisy joined in. "A princess promises to be pretty, peppy, smell nice, sparkle a lot, sing happy songs very loudly, and never, ever be mean."

When they finished the pledge, Francine smiled and gave Olivia a big hug.

"Olivia! It really *is* you!" she said. "But if you are the real Olivia, where is the real Princess Stephanie?"

It turned out that Olivia's family's car had a flat tire, which is why they didn't make it to the party. The king leaned out of the carriage and asked Dad if he could use some help. As soon as the carriage stopped, Olivia and Princess Stephanie ran into their mothers' arms.

"Mom," said Olivia. "I missed you!"

"Mumsy," said Princess Stephanie, running to the queen. "I missed you ever so much!"

Olivia's mom was confused. Then the queen explained that the girls had switched places for a day, and it all made sense. Before long, it was time for Olivia and Princess Stephanie to say good-bye.

"I had so much fun being you," Princess Stephanie said to Olivia.

"And it was *really* fun pretending to be you," said Olivia. "Let's be friends forever!"

That night at bedtime, the real Princess Stephanie told the queen about her amazing day.

"I played with the dog, and I ate a sandwich on a paper plate. . . . ," she said.

At Olivia's house, the real Olivia told her mom all about her time at the castle.

"I rode a pony and had a tea party and even wore purple pajamas!" she said.

Their moms gave them a kiss and tucked them in tight, happy to have their daughters at home.

"It's good to be home," Olivia and Princess Stephanie said.

"Good night, my little princess," their moms said. "Sweet dreams!"

And *both* little princesses fell fast asleep.

OLIVIA™
Builds a Snowlady

adapted by Farrah McDoogle
based on the screenplay written by Gabe Pulliam
illustrated by Guy Wolek

"Something very special is happening this weekend!" Mrs. H. said. "Does anybody know what it is?"

Harold raised his hand. "My mom is taking me to get long underwear?"

"No, not that," said Mrs. H. as the class giggled.

Olivia raised her hand. "I know," she said, "It's the Maywood Winter Festival!"

"That's right!" replied Mrs. H. "And what or, should I say, *who* is the most important part of the winter festival?"

"THE SNOWMAN!" the class answered all together.

Every year someone new is put in charge of building the snowman for the winter festival. It is a very special honor.

"This year our class will be in charge of the snowman!" Mrs. H. announced. "What kind of snowman should we make?"

There were so many ideas!

"A snow clown!" suggested Francine.

"Twin snowmen!" suggested Otto and Oscar.

"A snowman who is perfect and small—just like me!" suggested Daisy.

Olivia had an idea. "I wonder . . . ," she thought.
"How about . . . a snow*lady*? The biggest snowlady
the town has ever seen!" said Olivia.
Everyone cheered. What a great idea!

The next day Olivia met up with Francine and Harold to build the snowlady.

"Thanks for helping," Olivia said to her friends.

"No problem," said Francine. "But what is *that*?" she asked, pointing to a loud machine that Ian and Father were tinkering with.

"Oh, that's my mom's cotton-candy machine," Olivia explained.
"Ian wants to sell cotton candy at the festival."
"Now let's get down to business," Olivia continued. She rolled out
a blueprint for Harold and Francine to see. "Here's the plan. . . ."

Olivia, Francine, and Harold got to work.
Harold went to find things to make the snowlady's face.

Olivia and Francine rolled some snowballs. The snowballs got bigger and bigger . . . until they were giant-size!

"Wow, these snowballs are huge," said Francine. "There's no way we can lift another snowball all the way up there!"
"Who said anything about lifting it?" replied Olivia. "We'll use a ramp!"

"Now prepare to launch!" Olivia called to Francine after they had constructed their ramp. Just as Olivia launched the snowball, Harold showed up, holding a big carrot and lumps of coal.
"Look out!" called Olivia and Francine. But it was too late.

Luckily for Harold, the giant snowball just rolled right over him. And as it rolled over him, it picked up the carrot and lumps of coal before landing softly on top of the other two snowballs.

"Wow, she's as big as a dinosaur!" said Ian.
"The snowlady is beautiful," added Father.
"Building a snowlady is hard work. Great job, everyone," Olivia said.

The next day was the day of the festival. Olivia woke up feeling very excited.

"Look alive everybody! Grab your mittens and scarves! We have to get to the festival!" said Olivia as she rushed into the kitchen.

Then Olivia looked out the window and saw that it was a very sunny day outside. Very sunny indeed.

"Uh-oh," said Olivia.

Later, at the festival grounds, Olivia looked around for the beautiful snowlady. At first she couldn't find her . . . and then she spotted her.

"What happened to the snowlady?" asked Harold.

"She melted," said Olivia.

"Oh, no!" cried Francine.

"What will we do?" asked Harold.

In the distance Olivia's father fired up the cotton-candy machine, and it gave Olivia a wonderful idea.

"Harold, Francine, we're building a bigger, better snowlady!" she said excitedly.

"But the snow is too slushy!" Francine pointed out.

"Who needs snow?" Olivia exclaimed. "We have something better!"

"The thing about cotton candy," Olivia explained to her friends, "is that you have to twirl it!"

Olivia twirled and twirled.
Francine twirled and twirled.

Harold twirled . . . and got dizzy.
So Ian helped out and twirled.

"All right, twirlers, that should do it!" Olivia called. Then she whistled and moments later, Perry appeared with Olivia's trunk on a sled. "And now to put it all together!" Olivia told her friends. Soon the cotton-candy snowlady had a face made of rubber-ball eyes and a watermelon mouth. A tinfoil tiara sat on top of her head. She towered over the crowd that had gathered.

"Ladies and gentlemen, I present to you the world's biggest and *pinkest* snowlady!" Olivia exclaimed.

Everyone oohed and aahed.

"This is the most magnificent snowlady I have ever seen!" said Mrs. H.

"And the tastiest," added Harold.

"Let the winter festival begin!" cried Olivia.

Later that night, it was time for bed.

"Olivia, that was the best winter festival ever, thanks to you and your snowlady," said Olivia's mother.

"Thanks, Mom," said Olivia. "I think I'll make a cotton-candy igloo next! Or maybe a cotton-candy cruise ship . . ."

"That sounds wonderful," replied Mother. "I can't wait for next year's festival. Good night, Olivia."

OLIVIA™
Meets Olivia

adapted by Ellie O'Ryan

based on the screenplay "The Two OLIVIAS" written by Pat Resnick

illustrated by Art Mawhinney and Shane L. Johnson

Ring! Ring! Ring!
Mrs. Hoggenmuller rang her cowbell three times, like she did every morning.

Olivia sat up very straight, like she did every morning.
School was about to start, and Olivia, like always,
was ready!

Mrs. Hoggenmuller stood at the front of the class. A new classmate stood next to her. "Good morning, children," Mrs. Hoggenmuller said. "We have a new student joining our class today."

A new student! Olivia was so excited! "Can the new girl sit next to me?" she asked.

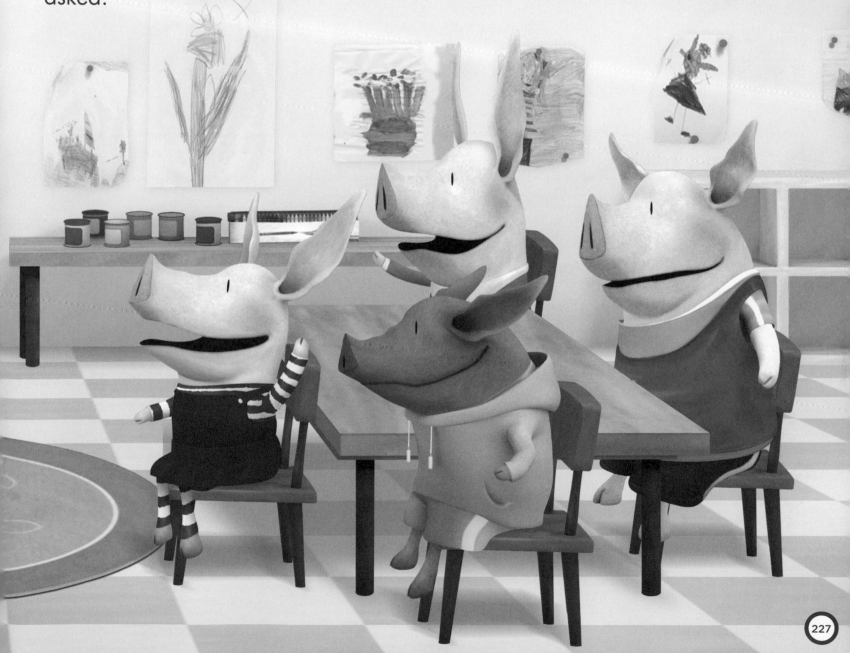

"That would be very nice, Olivia, because you two have a lot in common," Mrs. Hoggenmuller said. "In fact there's something about you that is absolutely identical. Olivia, meet Olivia!"

Olivia's smile disappeared. "But *my* name is Olivia!" she said.

"You're *both* named Olivia," replied Mrs. Hoggenmuller, turning to face the chalkboard. "Now it's time for math. Who knows what four plus two is?" Both Olivias waved their hands in the air.

"Yes, Olivia," Mrs. Hoggenmuller said. But *which* Olivia did she mean?

"She was looking at *me*," Olivia said.

"But she pointed at *me*," the new Olivia said.

"From now on, Olivia will be Olivia One, and our new Olivia will be Olivia Two," Mrs. Hoggenmuller decided.

Olivia couldn't believe it. She had a new girl in her class, a new desk mate, and a new nickname—and it wasn't even lunchtime yet!

After school Olivia had lots of questions. So she found someone who had lots of answers—her dad.

"How can there be anyone else named Olivia?" she asked. "It isn't fair. Her parents didn't ask if they could use my name!"

Olivia's dad smiled. "But it's a good thing! It means a lot of people like the name. Every year more people name their babies Olivia. Maybe one day *everybody* will be named Olivia!" he joked.

Olivia imagined sitting in the kitchen with her family . . .

"*Please pass the salt, Olivia,*" *Mom says to Dad.*

"*This is a really good dinner, Olivia,*" *Ian says to Mom.*

Ding! Dong! goes the doorbell.

"*Package for Olivia!*" *calls the mailman.*

"*That's me!*" *the entire family replies.*

. . . Olivia shuddered. It would be *terrible* if everyone were named Olivia!

The next day at school, the confusion over the two Olivias continued. "Your turn, Olivia," called Daisy from the slide. But she was talking to the *other* Olivia.

"I'm having a playdate with Olivia!" Francine exclaimed. But she was talking about the *other* Olivia.

When Mrs. Hoggenmuller passed back the class art projects, she accidentally switched the two Olivias' projects.

"You got mine by mistake," Olivia said.

"I like yours better," Olivia Two said. "Let's trade!"

"But I'd like to take my drawing home," Olivia protested.

"Hey! Don't be mean to Olivia Two, Olivia One!" Francine said.

Olivia sighed. Two Olivias in the same class just wasn't going to work.

That afternoon Olivia made a big announcement. "Mom," she said, "I've decided something important. I'm changing my name to Pam!"

"Why would you do that?" asked her mom.

"Because I don't know any other Pams," explained Olivia. "I'd be the only one."

"Well, if you want to call yourself Pam, you can," Mom said.

"Okay!" Olivia exclaimed. "Pam it is."

Pam told *everyone* at school about her new name—her friends,
Mrs. Hoggenmuller, and even Olivia Two.
"Who knows how many days there are in the week?" Mrs. Hoggenmuller
asked. "Olivia?"
Pam and Olivia Two answered at the same time.
"Olivia Two gets a gold star!" Mrs. Hoggenmuller said.
"But I had my hand up first!" said Pam.
"She called on Olivia," Olivia Two said. "*Your* name is Pam."

During recess Pam did a lot of thinking. "I don't know if Pam is the right name for me," she said to Julian.

"You don't want to be called Pam anymore?" asked Julian.

"I just don't feel very Pam-ish. But I always feel Olivia-ish!" she replied.

"Definitely," agreed Julian. "You're definitely Olivia-ish!"

Olivia was very happy to be Olivia once more. After school she rushed up to her mom. "I decided to be an Olivia again!" she announced.

"I'm so glad," Olivia's mom replied. "All Olivias are special, but you're an especially special Olivia to me."

Olivia knew she had made the right decision to change her name back to Olivia.

But there was still the problem of the *other* Olivia.

What was she going to do?

Olivia imagined that she was in the Wild West, wearing a cowboy hat and a sheriff's badge . . .

"This here town just isn't big enough for two Olivias," Olivia says.

"Yeah?" asks Olivia Two. "What are you going to do about it?"

"We're going to have a duel," Olivia replies. "Whoever loses the duel clears out of town."

Each Olivia throws her ball high in the air—and catches it! Then they throw their balls even higher. Olivia Two reaches and reaches—and just barely catches her ball!

Olivia runs in circles, her arm outstretched. The ball lands in her glove. But then it bounces out!

Olivia dives through the dirt and catches the ball just before it hits the ground! "That was some catch!" Olivia Two says. She is very impressed.

"Your catch was pretty good, too," Olivia replies. "Let's call it a tie. From now on, this is a two-Olivia town!"

Olivia's daydream gave her an idea. Maybe there was room for two Olivias at school after all. Maybe they could even be friends! During recess she walked up to Olivia Two. "So how do you like our school, Olivia Two?" she asked.

"It's pretty good," Olivia Two replied.

"I'm glad you like it," Olivia said. She gave Olivia Two a big smile.

And Olivia Two smiled back!

"I'll give you back your painting, if you want it," Olivia Two said shyly.

"Thanks! I was thinking that maybe we should start an Olivia club, just for *Olivias*," replied Olivia.

"That sounds great!" said Olivia Two.

After school the two Olivias made a clubhouse for the Olivia Club.

"What should we do now?" asked Olivia Two.

Just then Ian poked his head in the clubhouse. "Hi! Can I come in?"
he asked.

Olivia shook her head. "No, this is a club for Olivias only," she said.

The two Olivias tried to think of something to do. Olivia didn't want to play
checkers. And Olivia Two didn't want to sing a song or play hide-and-seek.

"Hi!" called Francine. "Can I play?"

"No Francines allowed," Olivia Two said sadly. "Only Olivias."

The two Olivias looked at each other as they realized that all they had in common was the name Olivia.

"A club with just Olivias isn't very fun after all," Olivia One said.

The two Olivias agreed! So they ran off to play tag with Ian and Francine.

At bedtime Olivia had one more question for her dad. "Why do you think a bed is called a bed?" she asked.

"It's just a word that someone made up," Dad explained.

"Like Olivia is a word meaning me?" Olivia asked.

"That's right," Dad said. "Good night, Olivia."